For Max.
I love you to the moon and back.

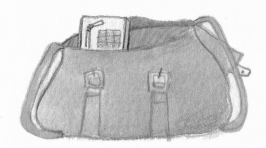

VIKING
An imprint of Penguin Random House LLC, New York

First published as *Tiger Lily* in the UK by Egmont UK Ltd., 2018.
This edition published in the United States of America by Viking,
an imprint of Penguin Random House LLC, 2020

Copyright © 2018 by Gwen Millward

Visit us online at penguinrandomhouse.com

LIBRARY OF CONGRESS CATALOGING-IN-PUBLICATION DATA IS AVAILABLE
ISBN 9780593118153

Manufactured in China

1 3 5 7 9 10 8 6 4 2

TIGER WILD

Gwen Millward

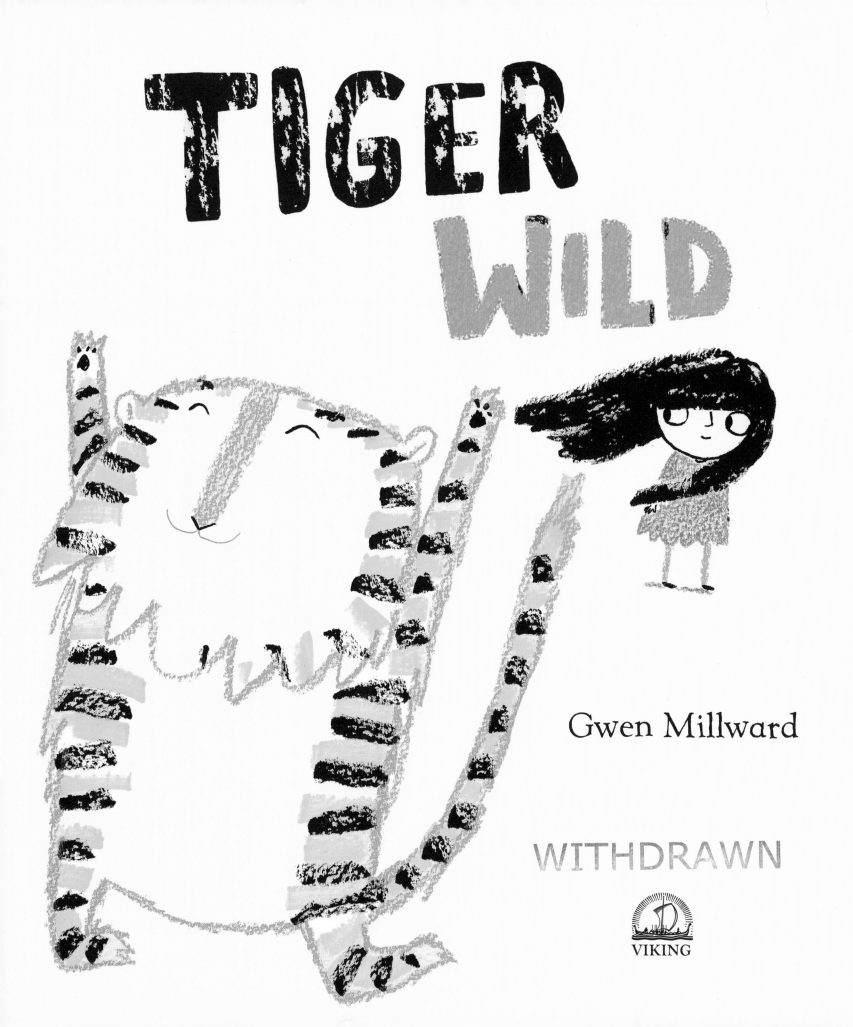

Viking

"*Tiger did it,*" said Lily.

"Tiger is very naughty," said Penny.
"Where is he?"

"Hiding," said Lily.

And it was true—

Penny couldn't see
Tiger anywhere.

But Lily knew he was there.

The next day, the special strawberry fairy cakes Penny had baked disappeared.

And then something happened to Penny's knitting.

"Did Tiger do that as well?" asked Penny.

"Yes," said Lily. "And he *isn't sorry*," she added.
Which was true, he wasn't.

"Well, Tiger is very naughty and will go to
his room until he says he's sorry," said Penny.

Tiger was listening.

He didn't like being told to go to his room.

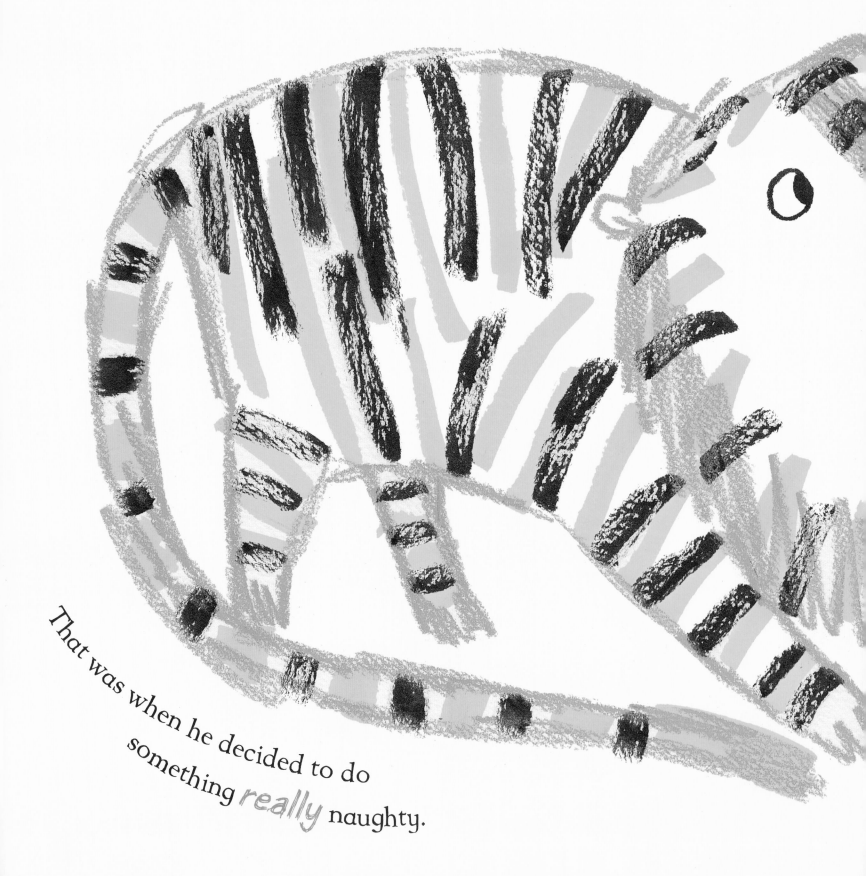

That was when he decided to do something *really* naughty.

"Come on, Lily," roared Tiger. "Let's run away and have some fun. We can do anything we want. We can be

Wild!"

Lily knew running
away was bad.
But she did it anyway.
After all, it was
Tiger's idea.

She tiptoed out of her bedroom
and packed a bag of important things:

a sandwich,   a carton of
              chocolate milk,

a pair of
binoculars,

and a map, so she could
find her way home.

"*Let's go!*" shouted Tiger.
"Let's **stomp** and *jump* and *make a mess!*"
Tiger wanted to do everything . . .

So they did.

They *stomped* through the long grass.

And they *jumped* in muddy puddles and made a big mess.

Being wild was fun. Tiger and Lily felt free.

"Follow me, Lily!"
said Tiger,
leading her deeper into the wild,
where the bushes grew thick.

Sometimes there were big scary
things, and Lily was glad to have
Tiger, who was never afraid.

But other times . . .

she wished he wasn't quite so *roarsome* and *wild*.

Sometimes Lily wanted to be quiet and still.

On and on they went, and Lily began to feel hungry. She reached into her bag for her sandwich . . .

but it wasn't there.

Tiger looked at Lily.

Lily looked at Tiger.

And then Lily realized . . .

the sandwich
was in Tiger!

So were the
chocolate milk
and the binoculars!

And worst of all . . .
the map!

"I'll never find my way back!" cried Lily.

But Tiger thought
that was a good thing.

"We can be *wild
forever!*" he roared.

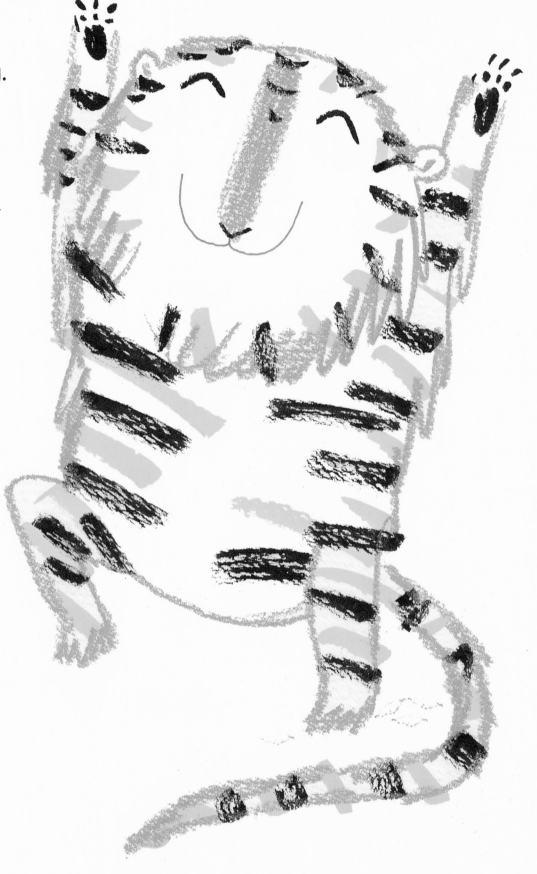

And then Tiger did something *really bad* . . .

he *ate* Lily's shoes!

"*Stop it, Tiger!* You're too naughty! **Go away!**" shouted Lily. She didn't want to always be like Tiger. She didn't want to be wild forever. So she ran.

Lily missed Penny. She knew Penny would be missing her, too, even if she was still angry.

It was getting dark. *Scary* night things were about.

The wild was getting *wilder*
and Tiger was nowhere to be seen.

In fact, Tiger didn't seem to be there at all.

Suddenly Lily heard a rustle in the grass.
But it wasn't Tiger . . .

It was Penny.

They hugged.

Then hugged some more.

"Tiger shouldn't have taken me into the wild
without telling you," said Lily, "and Tiger is sorry."

And he was very sorry.

"He's sorry for being
naughty, too," said Lily.

And he was.
Very, very sorry.

"Can we go home now?" asked Lily.

So they did.

Penny wrapped Lily in a big blanket.
And Lily wrapped up Tiger next to her.

After that day, Tiger and Lily did sometimes go to the wild together. But they never went for long. And they never went without telling Penny.

And sometimes . . .

Penny went too, because there's a time to be quiet and still and a time to be

wild and free!